Tomie de Paola's
KITTEN KIDS™
and the Haunted House

A GOLDEN BOOK · NEW YORK
Western Publishing Company, Inc., Racine, Wisconsin 53404

"Race you!" shouted Katie to Kit. "I'll beat you to the house at the end of the block!" And before her little brother could stop her, Katie was off and running as fast as she could go.

Kit loved to have races with Katie, even though he almost never beat her. In fact, the only times he won were when she let him.

He remembered the time Katie and her friends pretended to race him to the other side of Catfish Creek. He got there first, but he looked like a mudball!

Mama and Papa had scolded Katie for tricking him.

Kit didn't want to race Katie today. He was afraid of the house at the end of the block. No one had lived in it for a long time. Kit was sure it was haunted.

"Wait, Katie!" he called. But she was too far ahead of him to hear.

"Come back, Katie!" he shouted again. When she didn't turn around, he gave up and ran after her.

Grandma and Grandpa lived on the same block as Katie and Kit. When Kit ran past their house, he thought about stopping. Grandma would have a treat for him. Grandpa would tell him a story.

But if he stopped, Katie would not know where he was. So he kept on running.

At the end of the block Kit slowed down. In front of him was the haunted house. And there was no sign of Katie.

Kit saw something move in the bushes near the house.
A bird flew out and scared him! But there was no Katie.
Kit looked around the side of the house. He crept all
the way to the backyard. Still no Katie.

Kit was getting worried. Maybe there was a witch in the haunted house, he thought. And maybe the witch had caught Katie! What would Mama and Papa say if he came home without her?

"Katie," he whispered. But no one answered.

Where was she, anyway? he wondered. Up the porch steps he went, very slowly. There was a loud creaking noise, and Kit jumped into the air. He had scared himself!

As quietly as he could, Kit climbed all the way up the steps and onto the front porch. The porch was empty.

A window was open. From inside the house Kit heard a long, high laugh. It was the witch! Kit's hair stood straight up.

"Oh, Katie," he whispered.

Suddenly a wonderful fragrance drifted past his nose, and Kit recognized the smell of cookies baking in the house.

"Oh, no!" said Kit. The witch was probably planning to feed sweet things to Katie, he thought. Then Katie would get fat and tasty. And the witch would eat her up!

Kit pushed open the front door with all his strength and burst into the haunted house. He was not going to let any mean witch eat Katie up!

"Katie! Katie!" he called.

And he heard her answer, "In here, Kit!"

Kit followed the cookie smell through the living room and ran straight for the kitchen.

Katie was in the kitchen. A girl was with her.
"Kit!" said Katie. "Where have you been?"

Kit was so surprised, he couldn't say a word.

"This is Katrina," said Katie. "She's in my class at school. Katrina's family just moved into this house. Her mama said we could have cookies and milk."

"Hi, Kit," Katrina said. "Do you want some cookies?"

They were Kit's favorite, chocolate chip, but he felt too shaky to eat any.

"What's the matter?" Katie asked.

"Oh, nothing," said Kit. "I'll just take one for later."

Soon Katrina's papa came in and sent them all out
to play.

Kit was starting to feel better. "I guess the house isn't haunted after all," he thought.

He bit into the cookie. "Yum," Kit said. Now he felt good enough to beat Katie in a race.

"Race you to our house!" he shouted.

And before either of the girls could say anything, he was off and running as fast as he could go.